DATE DUE

Cabbages and Kings

a story by

Elizabeth Seabrook

paintings by

Jamie Wyeth

VIKING

VIKING
Published by the Penguin Group
Penguin Books USA Inc., 375 Hudson Street, New York, New York 10014, U.S.A.
Penguin Books Ltd, 27 Wrights Lane, London W8 5TZ, England
Penguin Books Australia Ltd, Ringwood, Victoria, Australia
Penguin Books Canada Ltd, 10 Alcorn Avenue, Toronto, Ontario, Canada M4V 3B2
Penguin Books (N.Z.) Ltd, 182-190 Wairau Road, Auckland 10, New Zealand

Penguin Books Ltd, Registered Offices: Harmondsworth, Middlesex, England

First published in 1997 by Viking, a division of Penguin Books USA Inc.

3 5 7 9 10 8 6 4 2

Text copyright © Elizabeth Seabrook, 1997
Illustrations copyright © Jamie Wyeth, 1997
All rights reserved

LIBRARY OF CONGRESS CATALOGING-IN-PUBLICATION DATA
Seabrook, Elizabeth.
Cabbages and kings / by Elizabeth Seabrook ; paintings by Jamie Wyeth.
p. cm.
Summary: Albert, the asparagus whose family has grown in Farmer John's garden
for years, and a newcomer, Herman the cabbage, spend the days from
spring until time for a fair getting to know each other.
ISBN 0-670-87462-0 (hardcover)
[1. Asparagus—Fiction. 2. Cabbage—Fiction. 3. Gardens—Fiction.]
I. Wyeth, Jamie, ill. II. Title.
PZ7.S43755Cab 1997 96-52795 CIP AC

Printed in U.S.A.
Set in Cochin

To Lisa Reed Seabrook

———— ❧ ❧ ————

who saw the first asparagus spears emerging alone
in our farm garden on a chilly spring day and exclaimed,
"My, aren't they brave little things!"

The smooth brown earth in Farmer John's vegetable garden seemed to be waiting for something. It was the first warm day of early spring.

A furry gray rabbit stood on his hind legs and peered through the fence. He saw there was nothing green to eat. "Too soon," he muttered, and hopped off through the fields to find his dinner.

A bird swooped down looking for a few seeds. "Too late," he chirped after he carefully studied the ground. The seeds had already been covered with a dusting of dirt so they would grow. The hungry bird flew off to nibble the buds of a cherry tree.

The day grew warmer, and suddenly something small and pointed and green pushed up right in the middle of the garden. It was the top of an asparagus spear.

"Whew!" said the asparagus, who called himself Albert. "I wonder if I'm first again."

He was, and that made him feel lonely. But as the warm sun came up each day, he grew taller. At last he saw other green tops nearby. His asparagus relatives were poking their heads through the brown earth. They looked unhappy.

"Cheer up," he called. "You'll be taller soon and able to look around the garden."

Albert tried to pull himself up so he could show them what he meant. For the first time he could look over the little hump of earth beside him.

"We have new neighbors," he called out. "And they're short and fat."

"We're cabbages," one of the neighbors growled. "And round is the way cabbages want to be."

"Tall and straight is the way asparagus wants to be," Albert replied, looking very pleased with himself.

"Wait till the wind blows and you get dust in your eyes," the cabbage answered. "Then you'll see who has the best shape."

Sure enough, that very night the wind swept down into the garden. The sandy soil was dry, and it began to blow across the asparagus patch, striking the bare sides of each stalk.

The cabbage hugged his pale green leaves tighter to his fat sides. "No dust is getting under my skin," he said loudly.

By morning the rain began, and Albert was miserable. He blinked the sand out of his eyes and looked at the cabbage. It was clean and shiny, its leaves curled over its head.

"Well, Fatso," the asparagus called unkindly. "You were right. I could use some leaves."

"Don't call me Fatso," the cabbage said crossly from underneath his leafy umbrella. "Can't we be friends? Call me Herman."

"Sorry," the asparagus said. "My name is Albert. I suppose there are some good things about being short and...ah...pleasingly plump."

"Thank you," Herman answered politely. "And it must be nice to be tall. You get to see more things in the garden."

So Albert began to tell his new friend what he saw growing in Farmer John's garden. He described the snowy blossoms on the pea vines and the rabbit he saw in the corner of the garden. The rabbit was hiding under a leaf of the rhubarb plant. When the farmer wasn't looking he would hop out and and eat some fluffy green carrot tops or baby lettuce or new cabbages. These were his favorite meals.

"The rabbit will be one of your problems," Albert warned his cabbage neighbor. "I'm safe, because rabbits don't like asparagus."

Herman looked afraid. "Tell me if you see him coming," he said, and Albert promised.

"Right now I have to worry about myself," Albert said suddenly. Two people were walking into the garden. They were Farmer John's wife and his little girl, Jenny.

"They're looking for something for their dinner," Albert said. "We're a very popular vegetable." He looked proudly down at Herman. "And spring is our season!"

The farmer's wife and Jenny walked down the row between the cabbages and asparagus. The little girl leaned over and stared at Herman while her mother looked carefully at Albert and his family.

"They have to grow bigger," Jenny's mother said. "We'll come back in a few days."

"I hope you noticed," Herman said, "that the little girl seemed to like me the best." He thought Albert had bragged a little too much about his family.

"She probably wants to take something to the county fair this summer," Albert said. "They give prizes for the prettiest vegetables. Last year she took two heads of lettuce and some onions. They didn't win any prizes."

Herman looked worried. "How do I look?" he asked. "Could I win?"

"So far so good," Albert said, "but look out! Here comes that rabbit."

The rabbit stopped in front of Herman. His teeth looked very big.

"Try to look tough," Albert whispered. "Rabbits like tender things."

Herman tried to make his leaves look tough, and suddenly the rabbit wiggled his nose and hopped across to the pale green leaves of new lettuce.

"Whew!" exclaimed Herman.

"Well done," Albert said kindly. "You can't have any holes in your leaves if you want to win a prize at the fair."

"I'll try," Herman promised. "By the way, how do you know so much about the garden. Aren't you new here, too?"

"My family's been growing here for years," Albert explained. "You see, once asparagus is planted it comes back every year for a long time. Now you cabbages come and go—here one year and someplace else next summer—depending on where your seeds get planted."

The days got warmer and Herman grew rounder while Albert got taller. Farmer John's wife and Jenny came almost every day.

The asparagus basket over the farmer's wife's arm got filled several times as she walked along cutting asparagus for the family's meals. But she never got to the end of the row where Albert grew.

"Wow, that was close!" Albert said one day as she turned back to the house. "Maybe she thinks I'm too tall."

"Never going to be my problem," Herman sighed.

"Actually, you're looking especially well these days," Albert said. "How do you feel?"

"Absolutely delicious," Herman replied. "Round and firm and fully packed. On the other hand, you're looking a little...ah...seedy."

Albert agreed quite happily. His head was sprouting tiny seeds at the top.

"Now I'll be left here till cold weather," he said. "I'm not so tasty when I start going to seed. And anyway, they always let some of us go to seed. It has something to do with making us stronger for next year. Later my seeds will sprout into a feathery bush. First it's green and then it turns a golden color."

"Like a king's crown?" Herman asked.

"Yes, but my crown is really ferns, not gold," Albert admitted.

"What about me?" Herman asked. "Would I get a crown if I stayed here long enough?"

"I'm afraid not," Albert said. "But by the time I get a golden crown I'll also have very cold feet, because it will be almost winter. And anyway," he added, feeling a little bit jealous, "you may get to go to the fair."

Early the next morning the rabbit hopped over beside Herman. He looked hungrily at his round green sides. But before he could take a bite a loud noise made the rabbit jump. A small brown and white dog raced into the garden, barking angrily. The rabbit started toward the fence with a giant hop.

"Look out!" called Albert. "That dog doesn't care where he steps."

Albert squeezed his eyes shut as the dog ran past, kicking dirt over the asparagus and cabbage. Herman peeked out from beneath his biggest leaf.

"Will he catch the rabbit?" he asked.

"He hasn't caught him so far," Albert said. "That's the farmer's dog, and he loves to chase rabbits. But that is one speedy bunny."

Farmer John's wife came into the garden, looking angry. She didn't like it when the family dog ran across her garden. She walked over to the cabbage patch, turning her back on Albert, and leaned down to look at Herman.

"I wonder," she whispered to herself. "I hope it's not getting too hot."

"What's this 'too hot' stuff?" Herman asked his friend, looking quite unhappy.

Albert explained that neither of them were at their best when the days and nights got very hot. That's why they were always the first to start growing in the garden. "Now corn," he added, "loves hot weather." Tall rows of corn nodded nearby.

"I guess it's now or never for me," Herman said. "That is, if I'm going to go to the fair."

That very afternoon Jenny and her mother came into the garden with Farmer John. They all leaned over and looked very carefully at Herman.

"Yep, this is the best one," Farmer John said. "We'll wait till tomorrow just before you go to the fair to pick the cabbage. It needs to look very fresh for the judges."

Albert and Herman could hardly wait till morning, although Herman was sorry not to stay around to see Albert's golden crown.

"You're my first cabbage friend," Albert said as the sun was coming up. "I hope some of your family gets planted near me next summer. It's been a pleasure knowing you."

When Jenny and Farmer John came the next morning, Jenny held the cabbage very carefully while her father gently cut away the stem that held it in the ground.

"Good luck at the fair," Albert called. Herman was looking very pleased with himself.

Albert looked around the garden and sighed. He was feeling lonely again. He wished he could have gone to the fair, too, but he had never heard of any of his family going to a contest.

Luckily Farmer John's wife and Jenny came into the garden the next day to pull some weeds from the green beans near Albert, so he heard the good news.

"Your daddy was very proud of your cabbage winning the blue ribbon," Jenny's mother told her. "Next year I'll let you plant your very own vegetable garden."

Albert felt almost as happy as if he had won a prize, too. He could imagine Herman with the first-prize ribbon.

When the summer days ended the garden began to look very empty. Albert's ferny top turned into a golden crown, and he shivered in the cold wind.

"Time for our winter nap," he called to the other asparagus. They began to yawn.

When the first snowflakes drifted down, the whole asparagus family was fast asleep. Albert was dreaming of cabbages. They all looked like Herman with a big blue ribbon hanging on him.